MW00892337

The Safe Return

By Ashley Wheelock and Arwen Evans
Illustrated by Abigail Gray Swartz

For my kids and my husband, and for Alli who is always cheering me on. -AGS

For my family, who help me keep my balance. -AW

To my husband Morgan and all others working hard today
and every day to help kids safely learn, play and grow. -AE

2020 Scotts Valley, California

ISBN Numbers:
978-1-7331374-5-4 (Hardcover)
978-1-7331374-6-1 (Paperback)
978-1-7331374-8-5 (Paperback Mask Only Version)
Library of Congress Number:
2020912831

Text Copyright Ashley Wheelock and Arwen Evans, All Rights Reserved
Illustrations Copyright Abigail Gray Swartz, All Rights Reserved

Feet on pavement.
Tush in seat.
Kick, balance, roll.

Haven't seen my friends in FOREVER.

Safety first. Travis waits.
One basket, one bunny. All set.

TOGETHER, but apart, we kick, balance, roll.
Feet push down, wind rushes up.
Dad jogs. I wave him back.

Nia leaps on her bike.

Goodbye!

Sibling, Riley, trails behind.
Their mom waves. Dad nods. Bells ring.

We are a pack. Five bikes split the sidewalk.
Ten feet propel us.

Kick, balance, roll.
I'm the leader.

The Hill. I. Can't. Stop. Now.

Oh no...

Hands meet ground. Tears fill eyes.

But my cries are not the loudest...

Five heads turn.
One basket. One upset brother.
No bunny in sight.

This is important.

Bike up, knees brushed, Daddy kissed.
Then I'm off.

We spread out further. Skim the pavement's edge.
Feet a chorus of drums. Eyes scan.
Low in the bushes, in a halo of flowers, a bunny waits.

But it's not THE one.

Back up the hill. It's tough.
Feet pound ground, we crawl forward.
At the crest, I point…

One bunny. Cuddle worn. Safely returned.

Kick, balance, roll.

Whoosh

Made in the USA
Coppell, TX
19 September 2020

38189122R00017